CHI 2/06

FRIENDS
OF ACPL

D1083512

Tara's
Tree House

Crabtree Publishing Company
www.crabtreebooks.com

PMB 16A, 350 Fifth Avenue,   616 Welland Avenue,
Suite 3308,   St. Catharines, Ontario
New York, NY 10118   Canada, L2M 5V6

For Miriam

H.D.

For Molly

K.L.

Cataloging-in-Publication data is available at the Library of Congress.

Published by Crabtree Publishing in 2006
First published in 2004 by Egmont Books Ltd.
Text copyright © Helen Dunmore 2004
Illustrations copyright © Karin Littlewood 2004
The Author and Illustrator have asserted their moral rights.
Paperback ISBN 0-7787-2743-2
Reinforced Hardcover Binding ISBN 0-7787-2721-1

1 2 3 4 5 6 7 8 9 0 Printed in Italy 4 3 2 1 0 9 8 7 6 5
All rights reserved. No part of this publication may be reproduced, stored in a retrieval system or
be transmitted in any form or by any means, electronic, mechanical, photocopying, recording, or
otherwise, without the prior written permission of Crabtree Publishing Company.

Tara's Tree House

WRITTEN BY

HELEN DUNMORE

ILLUSTRATED BY

KARIN LITTLEWOOD

Go Bananas

Chapter 1

TARA TIPTOED AROUND the corner of the house into the garden. She put one bare foot on the grass, then the other. The grass was long and cold and wet. In the tree the birds sang their early songs. Tara tiptoed forward. She was in the garden. She was really in the garden, walking on Mr. Barenstein's grass. Tara heard Gran's voice in her head.

"Now, Tara, you are not to go in the garden. It belongs to Mr. Barenstein. He has the garden apartment. He's old and tired and he doesn't want children in there running and shouting."

"I'm not running," Tara whispered to herself, "and I'm not shouting, either." She glanced back at the house. Everybody in the three apartments was sleeping. And Tara was going to go all the way to the bottom of the garden.

She tiptoed on. The birds sang a warning song.

"I don't care!" said Tara. "You can't stop me."

Suddenly she stood still. She listened. There was a sound, a creaking sound. Quick as a flash, Tara turned. She saw a window go up slowly. It was Mr. Barenstein's window.

He had seen her. He was going to open his window and shout at her so everyone in the three apartments heard. He was going to shout "WHAT ARE YOU DOING IN MY GARDEN, TARA?"

The window slid right up, and Mr. Barenstein leaned out. He looked straight at Tara, and at the long trail of footprints Tara had left in the dewy grass. But he didn't shout. He stared for a long time, and then he slid his window down.

Tara ran. She ran across the wet grass and around to the side of the house, through the front door and up the stairs to Gran's apartment.

She leaned against the inside of the door, panting. She knew Mr. Barenstein was going to tell Gran she'd been in the garden. Gran would be so angry.

"I want to go home," said Tara, but she knew she couldn't go home. She walked slowly into Gran's spare bedroom. There was Tara's suitcase on the floor. She hadn't unpacked it yet. Gran's clock ticked in the corner of the room. Six weeks, it said. Six weeks, six weeks.

"Shut up!" said Tara to the clock.

Chapter 2

TWO DAYS LATER it was the first warm day of spring. Tara put on her shorts, and stared out of the window at the garden, and thought about wading pools and picnics and running on the cool green grass.

"Please, please Gran, can't I go and play in the garden? Mr. Barenstein won't know. He's gone shopping, I saw him."

"No, Tara," Gran said. "Mr. Barenstein is old and tired. He needs peace. He's a good man."

Tara kicked the wall, just a little bit. She liked Gran. She loved Gran. But six whole weeks in Gran's apartment was a long, long time. And all because Mom was having a baby and her blood pressure was too high. Mom had to stay in the hospital until the baby was born. Dad worked on an oil rig, and he couldn't come home until after the baby was born. So Tara had to stay at Gran's.

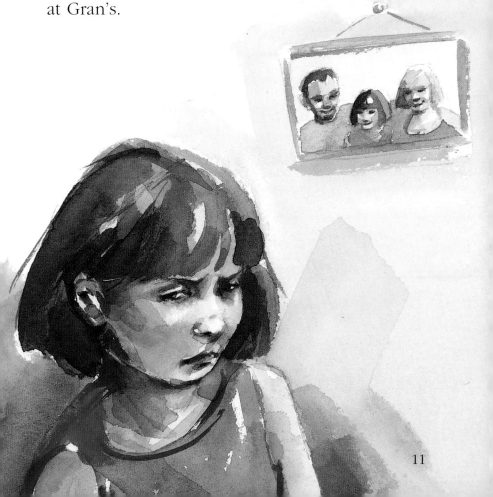

No Mom or Dad. No Jasmine, who was Tara's best friend at school. No walks with Billy, the dog next door. Tara kicked the wall again.

Suddenly the phone rang, and Gran hurried to answer it. Tara heard Gran's voice, but she couldn't hear the words. And then Gran was in the doorway.

"I've got such a surprise for you, Tara," Gran
said. Her voice was pleased and excited. "That
was Mr. Barenstein on the phone. He says he's
getting too old and too tired to look after the
garden. He wants everybody in the building to
use it and look after it for him. He says it's time
there were some children playing there."

Tara couldn't believe it. "Everybody? Does Mr. Barenstein mean me as well?"

"Of course he does," said Gran. "He knows you're staying with me, until the baby's born."

"So we can all go in the garden? Me and you and Mr. and Mrs. Giovanni, and Lisa when she comes to stay?" Lisa was Mr. and Mrs. Giovanni's granddaughter, and she was the same age as Tara.

"All of us," said Gran. "That's what he said."

"Gran, let's go in the garden right this minute!"

Chapter 3

THE SUN SHONE and the wind blew through the grass and through Tara's hair. It made Tara want to race all around the garden.

"Plenty of weeds here," said Gran. In one corner there was the tree Tara had always watched from Gran's window.

"It's an old pear tree," Gran said.

The pear tree was easy to climb. It had no leaves yet, but it had tight, rolled-up buds.

"Blossom," said Gran, looking up at Tara as she climbed. "We'll have pear blossoms soon, all over this tree."

Gran walked around the garden,
bending down as if she was
looking for something.
Tara sat on a branch
high in the pear tree,
and watched Gran.

"What are you looking
for, Gran?" she called down.

"A place for my garden," said
Gran. "I'm going to grow vegetables."

"Why do you want to grow
vegetables, Gran?"

Gran came and stood
under the pear tree. Tara climbed down and sat
on a branch just by Gran's head.

"When I was your age," Gran said, "I had to
leave my home."

"Like me," said Tara.

"Yes. But it was for a long, long time."

Tara thought six weeks was a long time.
"How long, Gran?"

"Five years," said Gran.

"Five years!" Tara nearly fell off the branch. "Didn't your mom and dad want you to go home?"

"Of course they did," said Gran, "but there was a war on. There were bombs dropping on London. Houses were being blown to pieces. If I'd stayed, I could have been killed. Mom and Dad had to send me away to the country.

Thousands and thousands of children were leaving London. Mom cried, but she said, 'It's for your own good, Annie. I want to keep you, but you've got to go.' So off I went to a safe place far away from the bombs. I went to a farm in Herefordshire, and Mrs. Floyd looked after me there."

"Oh," said Tara. "Did you like it?"

"I hated it at first," said Gran. "I cried every night. One night I ran away, but I got lost in a field full of cows, and Mr. Floyd brought me back."

"Was he cruel to you?"

"No. They were nice people. But they weren't Mom and Dad. Still, after a while I got used to it. I fed the pigs and collected the eggs and picked apples. Mrs. Floyd taught me how to milk the cows and how to make butter.

I went to school in the village. At first I thought all of the children talked funny, but soon I was talking just like them. And then one day I was out in the vegetable garden pulling up carrots and I realized I wasn't missing Mom and Dad anymore. I was happy."

Tara couldn't imagine being happy without her mom and dad. Not for five whole years. "Really happy, Gran?" she asked.

"Yes," said Gran. "I loved it all. The calves used to suck my fingers when I fed them, and every spring we'd have a couple of orphan lambs indoors by the stove. We used to give them bottles, like babies. The Floyds never had any children of their own, so they liked having young things in the house. They were good to me. But then, after five years, I had to come back to London."

"Why?"

"The war was over, you see. And you know, Tara, when I came back to London everybody at school laughed at me, because of the way I spoke. I was talking like a country girl by then, you see."

Tara swung on her branch, and thought. "It must have been horrible," she said.

"No. Not horrible," said Gran. "It was the war. War is a terrible thing, Tara. I was lucky nothing worse happened to me. Plenty of children weren't so lucky. Look, this is where I'm going to dig my vegetables."

Chapter 4

IN THE AFTERNOON, Mr. Giovanni took Gran and Tara in his van to buy vegetable seeds, a spade, a hoe, a rake and all the other things Gran would need to grow her vegetables. They cost a lot of money.

"I've got my savings," said Gran. Tara shook the packages and listened to the seeds rattling. On each package there was a bright picture. Gran bought lettuce, carrots, radishes, broccoli, peas, and beans. They put everything in the back of Mr. Giovanni's van, and Tara thought they would go right home. But they didn't.

"We'll buy the wood now," said Mr. Giovanni.
"I know a good place." He drove to a yard
where there was wood piled up everywhere.

"What's the wood for?" asked Tara.

"It's a surprise," said Gran. "Something I've
always wanted." Gran chose the wood with
Mr. Giovanni, while Tara stayed in the van.

Mr. Giovanni was a carpenter, so he knew about wood. Soon it was loaded into the back of the van.

"Please tell me what the wood is for," begged Tara, but Mr. Giovanni only smiled.

When they got home, Gran showed Tara the seeds from the packages. The peas and beans looked like real peas and beans, but dried up. Tara rolled them around on the table.

"Tomorrow Mr. Giovanni has to build in the garden," said Gran. "So we're going out for the day, to the mall. In the evening we'll go to the movies, and we'll have hamburgers afterwards. We don't want to stay at home and listen to all that banging and drilling."

It was dark when Gran and Tara came out of the restaurant the next evening. Tara was full of fries and cheeseburger, and she felt sleepy. "I can't wait to go in the garden tomorrow," she said. "I'm going to climb the pear tree again, only higher this time. Can I help you plant the seeds?"

"Of course you can," said Gran.

Chapter 5

THE NEXT DAY, TARA woke up early. Gran was still asleep. The curtains were closed in the living room. Tara pulled them back. She looked down at the garden. There was something different. Tara blinked. What was new?

Then she saw the pear tree. A little house had appeared in it, like a house in a story. A tree house. There were wooden walls and a roof. There was a rope ladder hanging down.

"A tree house!" whispered Tara. "A real tree house!" Then she ran to fetch Gran.

"How did it get there? Who made it? Who is it for?" shouted Tara. Gran laughed. "Mr. Giovanni built it out of the wood we bought," she said proudly. "You know, Tara, there was a tree house in an old apple tree at the Floyd's farm. I broke my heart when I had to leave that tree house behind. I said if ever I got a garden, the first thing I'd have would be a tree house."

"Is the tree house for you, then?" asked Tara in a small voice. Gran laughed again. "Can you see me climbing up and down that ladder? It's for you, Tara, and for Lisa."

Tara couldn't believe it. She hugged Gran as hard as she could. "I'll still share it with you, Gran," she said. "Even if you can't climb, the tree house can be half yours."

The tree house smelled of new wood. Mr. Giovanni had made a door frame and a window frame so Tara could look out and see what was happening in the garden. The roof sloped so that when it rained the water would run away.

"We'll look at the market for a little table and a chair," said Gran. "Then you can have your lunch up there if you want to."

Tara climbed up and down the ladder. She looked out of her window, and walked up and down the plank floor. It was perfect. It was all perfect. Maybe a bird will build a nest in the pear tree and I'll be able to watch it, thought Tara.

Just then Tara saw Mr. Barenstein coming up the steps from his garden apartment, leaning on his stick. He came up into the sunlight, blinking, and then he stopped to rest.

Slowly he raised his right hand. He beckoned
to Tara.

Tara wanted to stay in the tree house, but
Mr. Barenstein beckoned again. Slowly, Tara
clambered down the ladder, and walked across
the grass to Mr. Barenstein. He was smiling a
slow, creaky smile.

"Hello, Tara. You like your tree house?"
he asked.

"Oh yes! Yes! I love it," said Tara.

"It's a beautiful tree," said Mr. Barenstein. "Soon it will have blossoms."

Tara remembered how Gran had said the buds would turn into pear blossoms.

"I know," she said.

"In my garden, when I was a boy," said Mr. Barenstein, "we had a tree with blossoms on it in the springtime. A cherry tree. And one day my little sister Hannah climbed into that cherry tree. She was about your age, Tara. She climbed into the highest branches and she started to pull off the blossoms. Just like that, in big handfuls, all white. She threw the blossoms down over our mother, as if our mother was a bride."

"What did your mother do?" asked Tara.

"Well, she laughed. It was a funny thing. But she was a little bit mad, too, and she called to my sister Hannah, 'If you tear the blossoms, we will have no fruit.'"

"What did Hannah do then?"

"Hannah looked at our mother and she laughed and she tore down more blossoms. More and more white blossoms falling over everything."

"Oh," said Tara. She didn't want to ask Mr. Barenstein what happened next, in case his mother had been so angry that everything had been ruined.

"Yes, Hannah was your age," said Mr. Barenstein, looking down at Tara as if he saw someone else. "She looked like you, too. When I saw you there in the garden, I almost thought I was seeing my sister Hannah again." He leaned on his stick. He looked as if something hurt him.

Tara thought about Hannah. She had never known that Mr. Barenstein had a sister. And Mr. Barenstein sounded so sad when he talked about her. Probably Hannah was old now, much too old to climb into a tree. "Mr. Barenstein," asked Tara, "where is your sister now? Where is Hannah?"

For a long time Mr. Barenstein did not answer. Then he said, "That was a long time ago, Tara. It was in another country, far away. And then the war came."

"Oh, I see," said Tara. She didn't want to ask about Hannah any more.

"War is a terrible thing," said Mr. Barenstein. Tara stared at him.

"That's what my gran says," she said. But she wished Mr. Barenstein would stop talking about the war. She wanted to climb back into the tree house.

"Your gran is right," said Mr. Barenstein. He smiled his old, creaky smile again. "I shouldn't keep you, Tara," he said. "You want to climb up into your tree. Just like my sister Hannah."

Chapter 6

A LITTLE LATER, Gran came out with a plate of sandwiches and chips on a tray, and an orange drink with a straw in it.

"Guess what Mrs. Giovanni's just told me," she said. "Lisa is coming tomorrow. She's staying for a whole week. Lisa can't wait to see the tree house."

Tara couldn't wait either. She thought of picnics with Lisa up in the tree house. They'd all have a barbecue too, with burgers and sausages and marshmallows on sticks, and Mr. Giovanni drinking beer. Maybe Tara and Lisa could sleep in the tree house all night. They could bring their quilts and pillows and have a midnight feast and . . .

Tara thought of something else. "Gran. Did you know Mr. Barenstein had a sister called Hannah?"

Gran looked at Tara. Her face was very sad. "I know, Tara. He told me about her once."

"Mr. Barenstein said Hannah used to climb trees when she was my age. Right into the highest branches. Hannah looked like me."

"Did she?"

"She was in the war, like you," said Tara.

"Yes," said Gran. "It's like I told you, Tara. War is a terrible thing. Some children got away into safe places. I was lucky. But Hannah was in another country, and there were no safe places there, not even for a little girl like Hannah." Then she said, in a different voice, "I've planted the radish seeds, Tara. They'll be coming up in no time with this sunshine. Now eat your lunch." And Gran went back into the house.

Tara ate her sandwich and chips. She thought about Hannah, and Mr. Barenstein saying that Tara looked like Hannah, and about Gran going away from her mom and dad for five years, because of the war. Gran got away into a safe place, but there was no safe place for Hannah.

If Hannah was here now, she would climb high into the pear tree, just like me, thought Tara. I'd have someone to play with.

But there was only Tara in the garden. She looked out of the tree house window, and there were the tight, rolled-up buds. Soon the buds would open, Gran said. And tomorrow . . .

Tomorrow Lisa was coming.

"I'm going to phone Mom at the hospital tonight," said Tara to herself, "and I'll tell her about the tree house, and Gran's vegetable garden, and all the things that are happening in the garden. Six weeks isn't long really."

Tara leaned out of the window of her tree house and looked up at the sky. She thought of Hannah high up in the tree, laughing. There were puffs of cloud blowing past, just like Hannah's white blossoms.

EVACUEES

When Britain declared war on Germany in 1939, children were moved – "**evacuated**" – from big cities to the safety of smaller villages and towns in the country. These children were called **evacuees**. They were evacuated to protect them from the German bombing that was taking place in cities like London and Liverpool. Over **three million** children were evacuated during the war!

GRAN'S STORY: Mom and Dad took me to the train station. I was wrapped up like a little parcel, with my name and address on a sign around my neck.

I'd never been on a train before!

Look! A cow!

There were six of us traveling together on the train. A lady called Mrs. Malone looked after the little ones.

When we arrived in the country we all felt a little nervous, and very tired. A billeting officer told us which family we would stay with. She called them "host families".

Some children, like me, stayed for five years – for the whole war.

Many children loved their time in the country. But some were unhappy, and many went home to the cities, despite the danger. A lot of evacuees even spent birthdays and Christmas away from home!

PACKING TO GO AWAY

This is the suitcase I took with me when I was evacuated. The government gave us a list of things we should take. Here are some of them:

Gas mask
Woolly sweater
ID card
Ration book
Warm coat
Handkerchief
Socks
Shoes

Everyone had an identity card so police could check that they weren't a German spy!

NATIONAL REGISTRATION
IDENTITY CARD

Gran's sweater was knitted by her mom, from old wool.

Children had to carry gas masks with them everywhere, in case of gas attack.

There wasn't much food to go around during the war. So food had to be shared equally – "rationed". At one time, the chocolate ration was only half a chocolate bar a week!

Ration CHOCOLATE 2½°

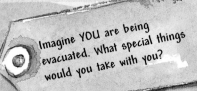

Imagine YOU are being evacuated. What special things would you take with you?

WRITING HOME

The Floyds didn't have a telephone, and there were no cell phones or email then. So I used to write to my mom and dad every week. Here's one of my letters.

March 1940

Dear Mom and Dad,

Thank you for your letter. I am fine. I like the country now. Yesterday me and Mrs. Floyd had a lovely day. We planted some seeds — we're going to grow carrots, lettuces, and beans! I went to look today, but they haven't come up yet.

I miss you both, and I miss Puss. Is Puss very scared when bombs drop? Mr. and Mrs. Floyd have a cat, too. I like her. She lives in the barn, and her name is Cat.

Do you think the war will be over soon? I hope so.

I'm sending you a picture I drew of Lucy the lamb. She's much bigger now!

Lots of love

Annie
x x x x x

Can you find two things that Gran missed from home? And two things that Gran enjoyed about living in the country?

Imagine what you would feel if you were evacuated to the country. What would you miss? And what would you enjoy?

Why not put yourself in an evacuee's boots? Pretend that you're an evacuee, and write a letter home. Tell your parents how you feel, and what you are experiencing.

DIGGING FOR VICTORY

During the war, growing your own vegetables was an important way of having extra food. The British government urged people to 'Dig for Victory' and to plant and harvest as many fruits and vegetables as they could. Even local parks became vegetable gardens!

Why not "Dig for Victory" and grow some seeds yourself? You don't even need a garden!

For their sake –
GROW YOUR OWN VEGETABLES

GROWING YOUR OWN FRESH SALAD:

You will need:
1 plate
1 piece of tissue or cotton ball
sprout seeds

Put a damp tissue or a cotton ball in a plate and sprinkle it with a few sprout seeds.

Keep them damp, and put them in a warm place, like next to a window, where they can get some sun.

In a few days, they'll have sprouted, and you can eat your very own home-grown greens!